friend [n] confidant, companion
Synonyms:
acquaintance, ally, alter ego,
associate, bosom buddy,
buddy, chum,
classmate, cohort, colleague,
companion, compatriot,
comrade, consort, cousin,
crony, familiar,
intimate,
mate, pal, partner,
playmate,
roommate, schoolmate,
sidekick, soul mate, spare,
well-wisher
P9-DMD-867

A Book of Friends

http://www.harperchildrens.com

Library of Congress Cataloging-in-Publication Data
Ross, Dave, 1949–
A book of friends / by Dave Ross ; illustrated by Laura Rader.
p. cm.
Summary: Discusses the different kinds of friends, what to do with them, and where to find them.
ISBN 0-06-028170-7. — ISBN 0-06-028362-9 (lib. bdg.)
1. Friendship—Juvenile literature. [1. Friendship.] I. Rader, Laura, ill. II. Title.
BF575.F66R67 1999 98-35266
177'.62—dc21 CIP
AC

Typography by Al Cetta
1 2 3 4 5 6 7 8 9 10
❖
First Edition

A Book of Friends

by Dave Ross
illustrated by Laura Rader

HarperCollinsPublishers

To my best friend, my wife, Kathleen

—D.R.

In loving memory of my mother, Lillian—

my first, best friend

—L.R.

Friends come in all different sizes and shapes and colors. . . .

You can have BIG FRIENDS

and SMALL FRIENDS.

It's not the size of your friends that counts.
It's the size of your heart.

OLD FRIENDS

When we were little...

Early readers

Birthday Bash

Pals forever!

Proud grads...

... proud Dads!

and NEW FRIENDS

It's fun finding out about new friends.

BABY FRIENDS

and GROWN-UP FRIENDS

Grown-up friends
aren't old. They're just experienced!

BEST FRIENDS

and FRIENDS WHO MOVE AWAY

Don't forget that

pen pals

can be great friends, too!

And of course,

IMAGINARY FRIENDS

There are all kinds of things you can do with your friends. . . .

HAVE A SLEEPOVER

GO TO THE BEACH

It's always a good idea to swim with a buddy.

GO FOR A WALK

SHARE

Some good things to share with a friend are cookies, books, secrets, jokes, food, clothes, hopes, fears, and other friends.

SEE A MOVIE

A good friend is someone who watches a scary movie with you and tells you what is happening.

HAVE AN ADVENTURE

It's fun to try new things with a friend.

JUST BE TOGETHER

If you just look hard enough,
you can find friends anywhere. . . .

AT HOME

Families make excellent friends.

NEXT DOOR

AT SCHOOL

Teachers can be friends, too.

ON VACATION

Stay in touch with your vacation friends.

IN A BOOK

Shh! Friendship at work.

AT THE PARK

You never know whom you'll run into.

UNDER YOUR BED

IN YOURSELF

Don't forget to be your own best friend.

A friend is someone who likes you, whom you like back.

Some people have a lot of friends, some have a few friends, some have just one friend.

It doesn't matter how many friends you have. Remember: It's quality, not quantity, that counts!

It's important to have friends. Friends make the good times better and the bad times easier.

Will you be my friend?

HINTS ON HOW TO BE A GOOD FRIEND:
Be a good listener.
Share your feelings.
Don't be afraid to say "I'm sorry."
Dear Buddy, I'm Sorry! Love, me
Remember all friendships have their ups and downs.
OW!